PUFFIN BOOKS

The Diary of Dennis THE MENACE

Canine Carnage

17

Collect all of DENNIS's diaries!

Other books by Steven Butler:

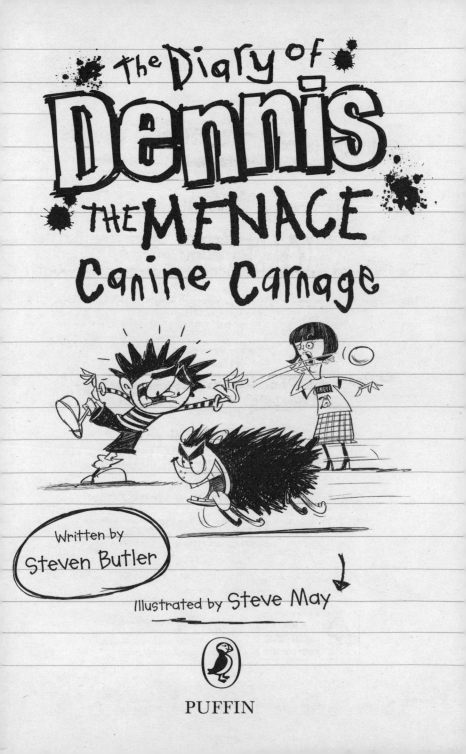

the Diary of Dennis the MENACE
Canine Carnage

Written by
Steven Butler

Illustrated by **Steve May**

PUFFIN

PUFFIN BOOKS

UK | USA | Canada | Ireland | Australia
India | New Zealand | South Africa

Puffin Books is part of the Penguin Random House group of companies
whose addresses can be found at global.penguinrandomhouse.com.

puffinbooks.com

First published 2015
001

Written by Steven Butler
Illustrated by Steve May
Copyright © DC Thomson & Co. Ltd, 2015
The Beano ® ©, Dennis the Menace ® © and associated
characters are TM and © DC Thomson & Co. Ltd, 2015
All rights reserved

Set in Soupbone
Designed by Mandy Norman
Printed in Great Britain by Clays Ltd, St Ives plc

A CIP catalogue record for this book is available from the British Library

ISBN: 978–0–141–35584–9

www.greenpenguin.co.uk

MIX
Paper from
responsible sources
FSC® C018179

Penguin Random House is committed to a
sustainable future for our business, our readers
and our planet. This book is made from Forest
Stewardship Council® certified paper.

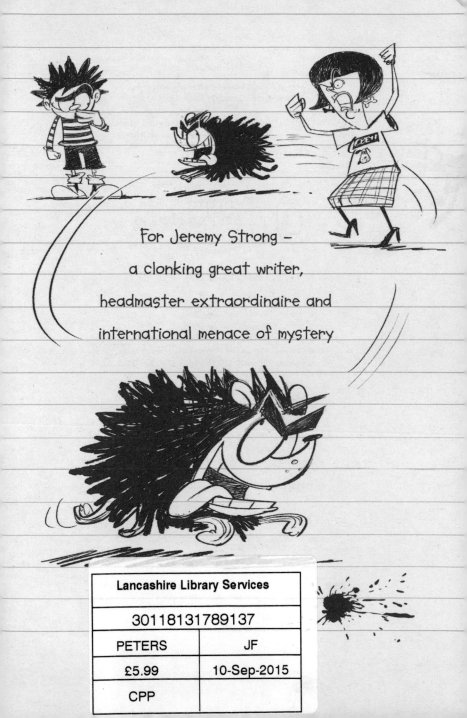

For Jeremy Strong –

a clonking great writer,

headmaster extraordinaire and

international menace of mystery

Just picture it, my Menacing Mates . . .

Close your eyes,
take a deep breath
and think of

MENACE-OPOLIS,

THE GREATEST CITY OF ALL TIME . . .
EVER!!! The funnest, COOLEST, most
menacing WONDERLAND in the WORLD —
scratch that — THE GALAXY! Ugh!

Double-scratch that . . .

THE UNIVERSE!!!!

And I'M going to build it.

Imagine walking through those

mighty gates . . .

I can just picture it now . . .
A MENACE-TOPIA filled with

video-game arcades, fairground rides, cinemas that ONLY show scary films, sweet shops, junkyards, LOUD MUSIC, circuses and burger bars serving my favourite SLOPPER-GNOSHER-GUT-BUSTIN' BURGERS!

It's going to be BRILLIANT!

Everyone will live in their own super-cool tree houses and right at the top, high above all the other buildings, I'll be the **EMPEROR** in my very own **TREE PALACE**!

Gnasher's tower

Treetop swimming pool with wave machine

Pea-shooter deck

MAMMOTH MEGAPHONE for shouting orders

Super-fast slide

Mega-swingy swing

And best of all . . .

SOFTIES WILL BE BANNED!

Not one boring, whining, wafty Softy in sight.

When I'm the emperor of MENACE-OPOLIS, I'll make sure that no **BUM-FACES** can ever come through the gates. I'll invent special SOFTY-SCANNER machines that will detect any **BORING-BRIANS** or **WHINGEY-WILFREDS** trying to smarm their way in.

BUT I ONLY READ WAR AND PEACE TWICE!

Oh no, wait - I've got a better idea . . .

Instead of banning them, I'll give the likes of Walter and his bum-faced chums, Dudley and Bertie, all the rubbish jobs that nobody else wants to do . . . like . . . **THE ROYAL TOILET SCRUBBERS!** Or the

Royal Fart Wafters whenever my little sister, Princess Bea, comes to visit! **OR** the **Royal Drain Un-blockers** after giving Gnasher his yearly bath! **Ha!** That would make my arch-enemy and all his cronies squirm . . .

It's going to be FANTASTIC!

I bet you can't wait to visit, have a wander

around and . . .

AGH!

WHAT AM I DOING?

CONCENTRATE, DENNIS!

You don't know **HOW** I'm planning to build Menace-opolis yet! Or about all the money I'm going to win, do you?

I'M SERIOUS, my Menacing Mates.

I'M ABOUT TO BE RICHER THAN RICH!

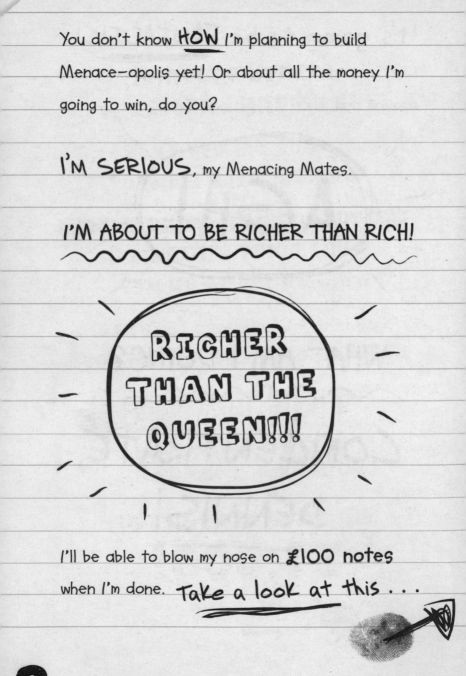

RICHER THAN THE QUEEN!!!

I'll be able to blow my nose on **£100 notes** when I'm done. Take a look at this . . .

ARE YOU A TOOTIFUL, BEAUTIFUL SINGER?

DOES YOUR GROOVY GRANDMA DANCE A MEAN MAMBO?

CAN YOU JUGGLE FLAMING SWORDS WHILE DOING THE SPLITS IN ROLLER SKATES ON ICE?

WHY NOT COME AND TAKE PART IN BEANOTOWN'S NEWEST TV SHOW,

THE FAME FACTOR!

WITH A GRAND PRIZE OF

£1,000!

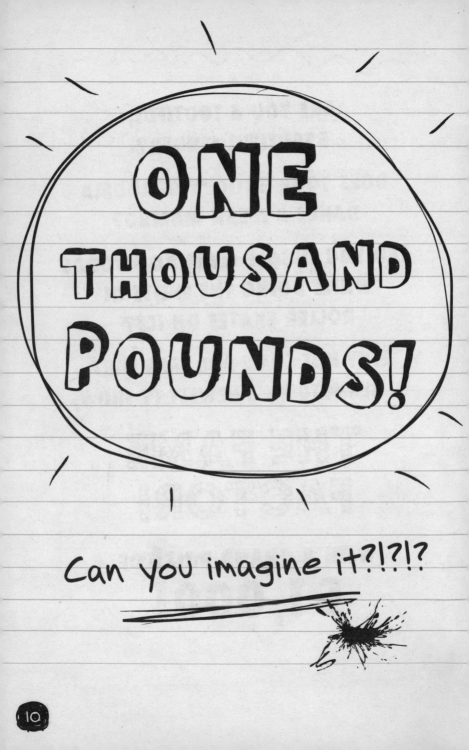

There's **NO WAY** I can lose a talent competition! Who in the **WHOLE WORLD** is more talented than DENNIS THE MENACE? No one . . . that's who! I'm practically stuffed full of skills and tricks. There's nothing I'm not **BRILLIANT** at . . . well, except being a boring **BUM-FACE** - I'M RUBBISH AT THAT! HA!

The only thing is, I have to figure out which of my talents is the best. It's just not easy when there are so many of them.

Ummmm . . .

MY LIST OF
MEGA TALENTS

- **Bogey** sculpture
- Whopping-Great-Mega-**Burps**
- Super-Fast-Ice-Cream-Eating
- Conquering Softies
- Shooting Things From Really Far Away With My **Pea-shooter**
- Flower-Bed-**Stomping**
- Squished-Bug-Collecting
- Whiff-tastic **Farting**
- Scary-Face-Pulling
- Marathon-TV-Watching

Hmmmmm . . . I just don't know.

All of those things are AMAZING menacing skills to have, but I need something to really, REALLY **WOW** the judges on The Fame Factor.

It has to be something that will

BLOW
THEIR
BONCES
OFF!

I need to have a really good think about this so I'll definitely be wanting brain food.

Luckily, I noticed a box of Mega-Crunch-Turkey-Tangles in the freezer. They're **MENACE-A-LICIOUS!** Especially if you cover them in ketchup before you scoff 'em down. Mum bought them for me and my best dog-pal, Gnasher, as a treat to say sorry for thinking I was the Bash Street Bandit.

I'll just grab a small portion of **Turkey-Tangles** . . . for medicinal reasons, of course.

HA! I can already feel my brain kicking into gear!

What did I tell you, my Trainee Menaces? I knew the Mega–Crunch–Turkey–Tangles would do the trick. Tasty, deep–fried, breadcrumbed, dripping–in–ketchup food always helps me come up with great ideas!

Me and Gnasher were pretty full so we wobbled off to bed to read comic books and let our brain food go down for a while. At first, nothing happened and I couldn't think of my best talent, but then I fell asleep . . .

AND HAD THE CRAZIEST DREAM!

It was genius!

I woke up with **ALL** the answers racing about in my brain!!! Let me explain . . .

My dream was pretty normal to start off with. Beanotown was under attack from CREECHER-BOT 3000, the giant KILLER robot-teacher from the BOOKY LAGOON, and I was SUPER DENNIS . . . flying through the air in my cape and stripy pants of power, fighting the rancid rust-bucket with my Mega-Zap-Gun and my trusty Laser-powered Pea-shooter.

When I finally defeated the Creecher-Bot, everyone came out of their houses, waving and cheering, throwing chocolate and money at me for being so brave and menacing.

AND THAT'S WHEN IT GOT INTERESTING!

All of a sudden, in my dream, my Mega-Zap-Gun turned into the coolest red-and-black-striped GUITAR! It was **FANTASTIC!** My mates Curly and Pie Face appeared out of nowhere and, before I knew it, we were playing the loudest, **MADDEST**, rockiest concert that Beanotown had ever heard.

I can't believe I didn't think of it before!?!?
It's just the thing to help me win the grand
prize . . . **MY BAND!**

Me and my Menacing Pals, Curly and Pie Face,
have the best rock band that ever existed.

WE'RE CALLED

The judges at **The Fame Factor**
auditions are special guests, and they're
bound to LOVE our KILLER rock music and
practically throw us through to the **LIVE**
FINAL ON TELEVISION. It's going to be
so **BRILLIANT!** I can just tell!

£1,000!!!!

With that much money, I'll be able to buy the
whole of Beanotown, bulldoze it to the ground
and build my own menacing wonderland in
its place . . . and put the toilets on top of
Walter's garden! **HA!**

There's a whole week until the auditions at
the town hall, so me and the boys have plenty

of time to rehearse and make sure that we're even ROCKIER than usual. We're going to blow them away with our **AMAZING** tunes.

AGH! I CAN ALMOST TASTE THE PRIZE MONEY!

Fancy-schmancy hat!

Pockets stuffed with money →

More money →

Solid-gold shoes!

EVEN MORE MONEY! →

MEGA-RICH MENACE!

Phew . . . that's better . . .

Anyway, my merry band of Menaces, I'd say it's about time we had a little catch-up. If you haven't had a sneaky peek through my other **TERRIFIC** diaries before, your fun levels must be dangerously low. How have you coped? You've missed out on some serious menacing. I feel so sorry for you . . .

The past year has been **MEGA MENACING!**

NO! EVEN MORE MENACING THAN THAT!!! I never imagined I'd be able to fit so many great menaces into such a small amount of time, back when I was first forced to write a diary by my EVIL husk of a teacher-fiend, Mrs Creecher.

She's THE WORST!!!

> You will write a diary for an ENTIRE SCHOOL YEAR!

I thought I was doomed when she told me I had to keep a diary as a punishment for not doing my summer holiday homework. I couldn't imagine anything more terrible! I thought I was a goner for sure . . . **HOW WRONG COULD I BE?** It turned out to be

MENACE-TASTIC!

What you're holding in your hands
is the fifth of my menacing manuals.

THE FIFTH!

I can't believe I've already filled
four whole notebooks with all the
MENACE-TASTIC things
I've seen and done. I should
get a medal for my menacing
contributions to society,
I really should.

If it wasn't for me, Beanotown would have been taken over by hordes of boring, flower-loving, fun-hating,

BUM-FACED SOFTIES!

Walter

Bertie

Dudley

CAN YOU IMAGINE?

That's not all. There's been loads of amazing and terrifying stuff as well . . . like . . . umm . . . **OH!** Like mystery Menaces terrorizing the streets, runaway hot tubs, sleepwalking

POP!
POP!
POP!
POP!

criminals, **GHOSTS**
and **<u>MONSTERS</u>**, LOOP-DE-LOOPY
rollercoasters, slobber-choppsy love letters,
exploding sandcastles, **demonic librarians,**
snowstorms, **AMAZING**
DISGUISES and
I even had to eat

<u>VEGETARIAN</u>
FOOD!

It's all been a whirlwind, I can tell you . . .

If you've read my other menacing manuals, you're well on your way to becoming a fully trained Menace by now. But never mind if you haven't. You'll catch up soon enough . . . It just so happens that tomorrow me and Gnasher are off for a **TERRIFIC**, menace—filled day at Beanotown Zoo, and it's a great place for you to start your training and learn all about being a tip—top

PRANKMASTER GENERAL.

YIKES! It's past midnight! We've got a busy day ahead of us tomorrow, my Trainee Menaces.

GOODNIGHT!

DON'T LET **BORING,** BOOKY **BUM-FACES** BITE!

Tuesday

10.30 a.m.: AND WE'RE OFF, my Menacing Pals. After three quick helpings of breakfast, me and Gnasher bundled up our sleeping-bags and then grabbed as many snacks, comics and bottles of DOUBLE-BURP-BUBBLE-POP as we could stuff into our backpacks. Beanotown Zoo, here we come! You'd love it!! It's one of the most menacing places in town.

I've loved it ever since I was a little Menace and Mum and Dad brought me and baby Bea for the day. There's a **SUPER-COOL** bit when you first come in and you drive your car through the baboon enclosure. **Ha!** I think the baboons liked Dad's car just a little bit too much . . .

Once a year in the summer, the zoo lets customers in for the whole night. **THE WHOLE NIGHT!** It's the most <u>MENACY</u> kind of sleepover you can imagine.

SCREECH!

HOWL!

<u>Yep!</u> Beanotown Zoo is a menacing marvel, full of the fiercest, most **fang-gnashing** animals from all around the world!!!

ROAR!

GRRRR!

Everyone arrives super early and waits for the gates to open. Then there's always a mad rush to get a spot near the enclosures with the scariest animals.

Well, let's face it . . . who wants to sleep next to the rabbits and gerbils in Princess Pixie's Petting Corner when you can bed down next to the **tigers** or **rattlesnakes**, or snooze in the **vampire bat cave?**

Only Walter and his wimbly-pimbly cronies want to sleep near the **cutesy, fluffy, cuddly** things.

Believe me, I should know . . .

I had a **DISASTER** last year. Ugh!
It makes my spine judder just thinking
about it. I'll tell you, but you'd better brace
yourselves, my Trainee Menaces. It was a

SOFTILICIOUS
NIGHTMARE.

I was on my way to Beanotown Zoo to meet
Curly and Pie Face for the sleepover when I
accidentally got distracted. I was minding my
own business, biking past Beanotown Burgers,
when I noticed a sign saying that if you
bought a SLOPPER-GNOSHER-GUT-BUSTIN'
BURGER you got a free chocolate-flavoured

SLURP-'N'-BURP-O-SHAKE! I HAD to
go in . . . No Menace worth their stripes
would pass up the opportunity to guzzle
down tasty drinks that make you

BURP!

I only stopped for a few minutes. After all,
it doesn't take the Prankmaster General
long to scoff down the tastiest burger and
milkshake in the UNIVERSE.

BUT . . . those few minutes cost me very
dearly, let me tell you.

When I got to Beanotown Zoo, all the cool
places were taken.
IT WAS TERRIBLE!

Minnie the Minx had grabbed the good spot on the bridge over the **Tiger Terrain**.

The Bash Street Kids had claimed the **vampire bat** cave.

Curly and **Pie Face** were in the insect house and hadn't saved room for me in all the excitement.

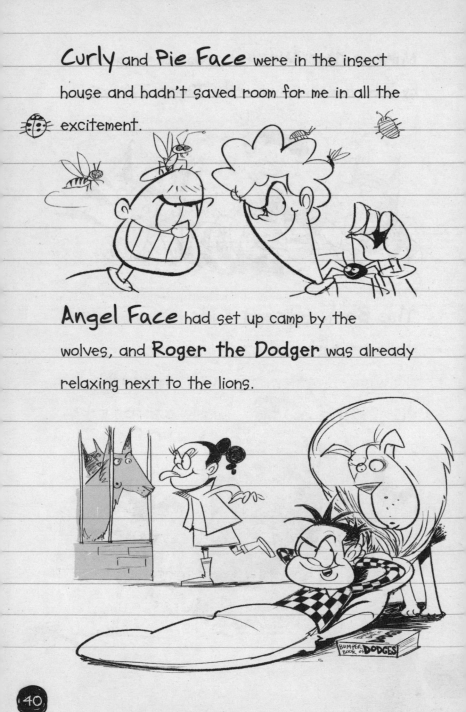

Angel Face had set up camp by the wolves, and **Roger the Dodger** was already relaxing next to the lions.

BUMPER BOOK OF **DODGES**

Even the **reptile room** had been grabbed by **Bea** and the rest of her pong-tastic playgroup pals.

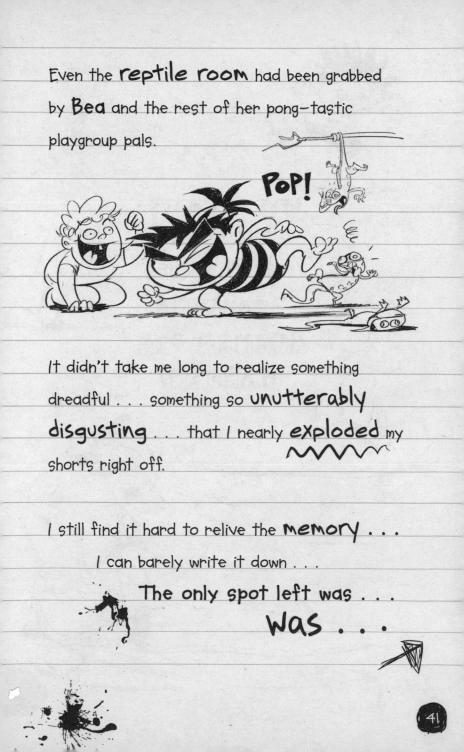

POP!

It didn't take me long to realize something dreadful . . . something so **unutterably disgusting** . . . that I nearly **exploded** my shorts right off.

I still find it hard to relive the **memory** . . .

I can barely write it down . . .

The only spot left was . . .

was . . .

NEXT TO WALTER,
DUDLEY AND
BERTIE BY THE
GIGGLING
GUINEA PIG
GARDEN!

All that boring baby stuff is miles away from the cool, menacing animals on the other side of the zoo.

It was **THE WORST**, my Menacing Mates! I had no other choice but to bed down right beside them! I missed all the best animals and felt like the laughing-stock of Bash Street School for ages afterwards. I couldn't show my face for days. Imagine it! THE INTERNATIONAL MENACE OF MYSTERY forced to pitch his sleeping-bag next to his archest of enemies in the petting zoo . . . NEAR THE GERBILS AND BABY GOATS!!! I've **never** been so humiliated in my life.

To make it even worse, I had to listen to Walter bawling all night because he thought a guinea pig had given him an evil glare.

But it's not going to happen again.

NO WAY!!!

Today, me and Gnasher are prepared and ready for action. I set my Mega-Bleep-Digi-Clock to wake us up MEGA early and we're off and out, armed with all kinds of menacing tools to help make tonight as fun as possible.

MENACING ZOO ESSENTIALS

- **Marshmallows** for sleepover snacking.

- **Camera** for cool animal photo opportunities.

- **Pea-shooter** in case Walter and his cronies pitch up too close.

- **Lion-repellent spray** (for emergencies).

- **Comics** for a spot of bedtime reading.

- **Double-Burp-Bubble-Pop** for drinky deliciousness.

The zoo doesn't open for another forty-five
minutes and there's already loads of people
outside the gates . . . I've just seen all the
Bash Street Kids, Minnie the Minx and
Angel Face jostling to get near the front.
Even my menacing gran's here with her pets,
Rasher and Gnipper.

Rasher

Gnipper

46

I'm glad we're prepared this year. Me and Gnasher **LOVE** feeding time the most. All that growling and pouncing and gnawing . . . **BRILLIANT!** That's why we HAVE to get a spot near the best animal enclosures. It's so cool watching the zookeepers feed the bears and lions AND SNAKES. **I CAN'T WAIT!** Maybe this year they'll see sense and feed Walter to the crocodiles? **Ha!** Actually, I doubt the crocodiles would eat him. He probably tastes like books and **BUM!**

12 noon, lunchtime: We're IN, my Trainee Menaces. Now it's a race to get to the best, BEST, **BESTEST** spot in the whole zoo.

I'M SO EXCITED!

I BET YOU HAVEN'T GUESSED WHAT
THE COOLEST SPOT IS, HAVE YOU?

Ok, I'll tell you . . .

THE BEST SPOT
IN THE WHOLE
ZOO

IS . . .

IS . . .

49

THE GLASS TUNNEL THROUGH THE SHARK TANK!

It's menace-tastic!

If you're first to pitch your sleeping-bag in the aquarium, you get to spend the whole night with **sharks swimming all around you!!!!** It's as if you're at the bottom of the sea!

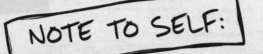

NOTE TO SELF:

ADD A ZOO WITH AN EXTRA-LARGE
SHARK TANK TO THE LIST OF
THINGS I'M GOING TO BUILD IN
MENACE-OPOLIS . . . AND ONLY
I CAN GO IN IT! **BRILLIANT!**

I can't think of a more menacing place to sleep
than the MIDDLE OF A SHARK TANK! We've
got to get there first . . .

Luckily, I planned ahead . . .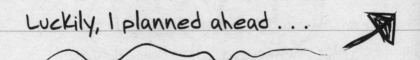

There is always a shortcut to be had.
No matter what, make sure you know
it. Your stripes may depend on it . . .

Me and Gnasher have been visiting the zoo
for days to scope out the quickest route to
the aquarium. While everyone else darts off in
different directions, we can take our time.

It's BRILLIANT!

LOOK!

WHAT DID I TELL YOU, MY MERRY BAND
OF MENACES?

WE MADE IT!!!

Me and Gnasher got to the shark tank in no
time. **HA!** It's going to be an **AMAZING** day,
I can tell. I can't wait to see the faces of
all the other Beanotown Menaces when they
come running into the aquarium and see that
DENNIS and his trusty pooch–pal are still

NUMBER
ONE!

Now that we've pitched our spot in the shark tunnel, we can have fun around the zoo. No one would dare to steal our place with our sleeping-bags there. It's part of the **Menacing Code** . . . and **NO** Softies would ever dare to sleep in the shark tunnel, so there's nothing to worry about from them. Now we can relax, knowing that tonight we're snoozing at the bottom of the ocean. <u>Yes</u>!

AAAAAAAANNNDDD . . .

it's not long before feeding time.

I CAN'T
WAIT!

AAAAAAAAAAAGGGGGGHHHHHH!

Something terrible happened, my Trainee
Menaces . . . It's nearly 8.30 at night
and I should be getting ready to settle
down among the sharks for the most
menacing sleep of my life . . . but where
am I instead?

AT HOME, THAT'S WHERE!

I just don't understand. It all happened so quickly . . . **it was a blur!** We were just minding our own business and then . . . before I knew it, me and Gnasher were back home . . . in trouble and . . .

And we didn't do anything wrong! Except . . . well . . . **UMMM . . .**

I'll explain.

There we were in the glass tunnel, getting
ready to watch the sharks eat. I was so
excited I didn't notice Gnasher sneak off . . .
and then just as feeding time started . . .

He's after the
SHARK'S DINNER!

The zookeepers in the aquarium threw a bit of a wobbly, but it wasn't Gnasher's fault. It was hours since our three helpings of breakfast and my poor dog-pal must have been hungry . . . really hungry . . . **REALLY, REALLY HUNGRY.**

Next we went to watch them feed **the lions . . .**

Then there were
the snakes . . .

NoooooO!

It went on and on like that until finally we got kicked out of the zoo by the **BUM-FACED** keepers! Who knew they were **Softies** all along?

Ugh! This is the worst day ever . . . **EVER!** Now I'm going to have to wait a whole year before I get the chance to sleep in the shark tunnel again, and it's all because of . . .

Because of . . .

Agh!

I can't be angry at Gnasher. He's my **bestest pal** in the whole of Beanotown, and who can blame him when there was all that food for the taking? Anyway, Mum and Dad can be angry at him instead of me.

They went bonkers!

Just after we arrived back home, there was a knock at the door. When we answered it, the manager of the zoo was standing there with a face like a smacked bottom. He handed a letter

to Mum and Dad, and kept wagging his finger and looking angry and babbling on about this and that and such-'n'-such . . .

YAWN!

I've never seen Mum turn such a bright shade of purple. It looked like her head was about to rocket off her shoulders when she read what had happened.

For Dennis the Menace's Parents,

I am writing to inform you of the dreadful,
greedy behaviour of your son's dog,
Gnasher. Zoo feeding time was completely
disrupted when that mangy mutt decided
to help itself to all the animals' lovely
mealtime snacks. It was Culinary Carnage!!!
I suggest <u>it</u> is taken to OBEDIENCE
CLASSES immediately. Next time this
happens, you will be paying the food bill for
every animal in Beanotown Zoo . . .

Yours sternly,

Albert Tross

Albert Tross
Zoo Manager

'IT'?! WHO IS MR TROSS CALLING 'IT'?

And mangy? No one talks about Gnasher like that. He's **not** mangy! He just needs a bath and has a particular knack for collecting fleas . . . lots of them . . .

Gnasher's the best dog in the **WORLD**. There's nothing he could learn at obedience classes that he hasn't already learned from me, THE PRANKMASTER GENERAL. A dog couldn't wish for a better trainer and a Menace couldn't ask for a better dog.

It's not fair! Grown-ups never understand . . . Don't they realize that I'm about to win the **BIGGEST** talent competition on TV and become a **MEGA-STAR**, and Gnasher is going to be the most famous dog in the world?

Mum and Dad sent us to bed without any **Double Fatties'** double-fat ice cream after dinner.

NONE! Not a dollop! Not a melty drip of the delicious stuff . . . **Such cruelty!**

Ah, never mind . . . I've got a few **Poppin' Jammy Sour-Candy Toaster Tarts** stashed under my bed. Me and Gnasher can snack on those later and forget about this whole sorry mess.

Ha! Gnasher looked so happy with all that exotic zoo food today. It was **BRILLIANT!** He might have ruined our night of sleeping in the shark tunnel, but . . . well . . . I'm proud of him.

Wednesday

10 a.m.: Guess what, my Menacing Mates!?!?
I think Mum is up to something.

Shhh!
Keep it a secret!

I crept down to breakfast this morning,
expecting her and Dad to still be in a proper
grump with me, like they usually are after I've
been in trouble. At first, I couldn't find either
of them, but then I heard Mum on the phone in
the living room.

She was talking to the Beanotown Vets and
sounded even snappier than usual . . . which is
pretty hard to do.

I sneaked up to the door and, by pressing my ear against it and listening carefully, I could hear her nattering away . . . Mum was moaning about Gnasher's bit of naughtiness at the zoo. 'A dog should never run away from its owner like that!'

Check . . . check . . . this is Reporter Dennis coming to you live from outside the living-room door. Mum is in a right strop and she . . .

Agh! She just said, 'I don't care . . . Gnasher deserves it after what he did!'

What are they going to do?

DESERVES WHAT?

BLLLUUUUGGGHHH!

She just said, 'That's the end of it. Gnasher will never be able to do it again. NEVER!'

Wh...Wh ... WH<u>AT</u>?

I think . . . I think they're going to . . . to . . . <u>AGH</u>! I can't even say it! I think Mum and the vet are going to send Gnasher away . . .

OR WORSE!!!

Dear Mum,

I **heard** what you and the vet are planning and I can't believe you would do such a thing!

All **Gnasher** did was steal a bit of **fish** . . . and **ham** . . . and **chicken** with **roast potatoes** and those little sausages with bacon wrapped round them . . . and a **banana sundae** . . . and <u>**stinky sardines**</u> from a few **selfish** **penguins.** I don't think they were even hungry . . .

You will <u>**never**</u> see me and Gnasher again. We're going to **run off** and . . . and

. . . 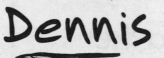 join the circus, live off bugs and twigs in Beanotown Woods, live in a mansion with solid-gold loos and a room just for burping in, after we win a squillion pounds on **The Fame Factor** . . .

AND I WON'T EVEN BUY YOU A CHRISTMAS PRESENT!

I hope your bum falls off and your arms shrink so you can't scratch it.

Yours sincerely,

Dennis

(formerly known as Your Son Dennis . . .)

OH . . . umm . . . I think I may have got a
bit carried away there.

Well, what was I supposed to think?

I just heard the next bit of Mum's
conversation . . .

Right!
THAT'S IT!
We're going to
get Gnasher
microchipped!

Gnasher?

Microchipped?

What's that? It sounds . . . It sounds AMAZING! There's me thinking they were going to do something HORRIBLE! I don't know what it means exactly, but imagine how menacing my best pooch-pal will be after he's been microchipped. He'll be part MENACING MACHINE! It's like Mum is rewarding us for Gnasher's bad behaviour.

MICROCHIPPED!?!?

I can't wait to tell Gnasher. He'll be the coolest dog in history . . . and think how **TERRIFIC** that'll make me, his Menace Master? I'll be able to scare the pants off Walter and every other Softy for miles around with a **robo-dog!**

I don't quite know what all this microchipping is, but I've had a good think and I imagine Gnasher will look something like this when it's all done.

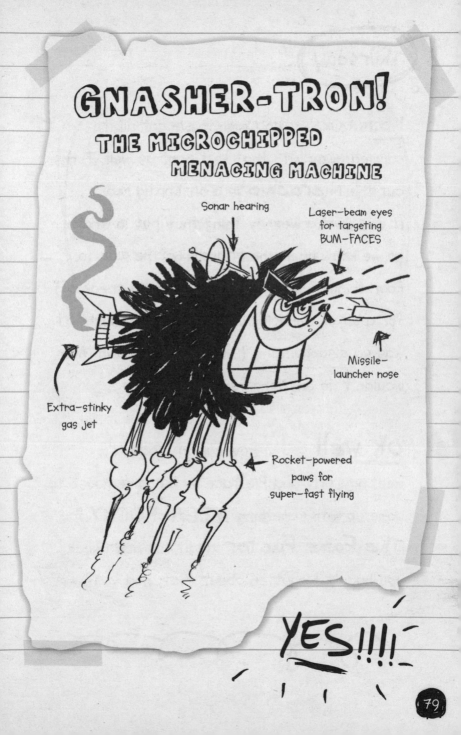

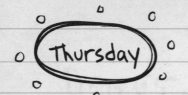

1 p.m.: OK . . . so I might have got a bit carried away with that last part as well. Turns out the **microchip** is a bit boring really . . . It was just a weensy thing they put in Gnasher so we know where he is and what he's up to. Poor thing, now he'll never be able to sneak off for a bit of menacing without getting caught. It was so disappointing. I should have known Mum wouldn't do anything fun.

Oh well . . . never mind. Today I'm meeting Curly and Pie Face in the tree house to come up with something **MEGA-ROCKY** for **The Fame Factor** auditions next week. You hadn't forgotten about that, had you?

We need a **ROCK-TASTIC** new song that's going to blow the judges' socks off and send us straight to the live final on TELEVISION.

Hmmm . . . I wonder what everyone else in Beanotown is planning for their big talent? One thing's for sure . . . none of them will be as **BRILLIANT** as the Dinmakers.

I've already been writing lyrics for our **KILLER** new song.

I'm gonna launch your **gr<u>an</u>y** into outer space. She's a **meteor-mama** with a wrinkly face!

WHAM!
BAM!
YOU SMELL LIKE
SPAM!

She's a **BUM-FACED** girl

In a **BUM-FACED** world.

Whatever you do,

Don't let her **breathe** on you!

Mutant **zombies** ate my brain.

Now I slobber and moan

And I'm **TOTALLY INSANE!**

We are going to win **The Fame Factor** for sure. Me and the Dinmakers are sounding rock-a-licious and we clearly don't have to worry about anyone else in the competition . . .

It was hilarious!

Me and the boys were in the middle of practice when we heard . . .

> Now come along, chaps. One more time . . . five, six, seven, eight!

There was no mistaking

that voice . . .

From the tree house, you can see most of the houses on my road. We peeked out of the window and, sure enough, there in Walter's front garden was **King Whingerella** himself with Dudley and Bertie. They were wearing the most stupid-looking costumes with long, floppy ears and doing some sort of dance. Ha!

The Dance of the Salty Prune Goblin is a wondrous thing!

Such majesty, Walter!

I think I need more bells . . .

THE DANCE
OF THE
SALTY PRUNE
GOBLIN!?!?

Is that the best old Walter-Wet-Pants can come up with? This is going to be so much easier than I thought. **Ah!** I can just see it now . . . The Dinmakers accepting their **Fame Factor** trophy and **£1,000** prize on LIVE TV!!! I'll be the envy of international Menaces EVERYWHERE!

Menace-opolis will be built
                        in no time!

Friday

9.48 a.m.:

NOooooOooo!!!!

NOooOooo!!!

NO-No-No!!

NO!

Just when things were getting better after the
Beanotown Zoo calamity, look what Dad left on
the kitchen table this morning . . .

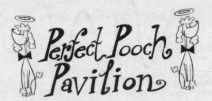

Perfect Pooch Pavilion

Dearest Dog Owner,

Thank you so much for writing to enquire about obedience classes for your Abyssinian wire-haired tripe hound, Gnasher. I'm sure he is a delightful dog and we couldn't be happier to welcome him to the Perfect Pooch Pavilion with open arms and a warm smile.

Gnasher will be an obedient bundle of joy in no time at all.

I look forward to seeing him and his owner for classes over the weekend.

Many thanks,

Olivia Pidd

Olivia Pidd
Dog Trainer

How could Dad sign Gnasher up for obedience classes without telling me? **GNASHER IS OBEDIENT** . . . sort of . . . **Parents can be so sneaky** . . .

I don't have time to skip about in class with Gnasher while he learns how to roll over and beg and let loose **rose-scented farts**. I need to be practising with the boys. We've only got a few days before the auditions.

NOTE TO SELF:

Mum and Dad will be **banned** from Menace-opolis!

The Next Day

I'M SO BORED!

This is torture,

my Menacing Mates.

Dad burst into my room this morning and told me that if I didn't take Gnasher to the Perfect Pooch Pavilion he'd never drive me and my little sister Bea to **Beanotown Burgers** again for as long as we live.

I couldn't do that to my little sister . . . She's such a promising Menace in the making, and a life without SLOPPER–GNOSHER–GUT–BUSTIN' BURGERS would stunt her menacing momentum for certain . . .

I HAD NO CHOICE!

So here I am . . . I can feel Boredom-Brain-Rot setting in for sure. There's no hope, my merry Menaces, I'm a goner this time.

Olivia Pidd, the dog trainer, keeps saying Gnasher will be a bundle of jowly-joy in no time. A bundle of joy? Gnasher is a bundle of something, but it's definitely not **JOY!** Not for the dog trainer anyway! <u>**HA!**</u>

<u>**2 p.m.:**</u> Olivia Pidd has been trying to train me and Gnasher for hours and **NOTHING'S** <u>**WORKING.**</u>

Now, Dennis, stand up straight, shoulders back and say, 'ROLL OVER!'

ROLL OVER, GNASHER!

Z
Z Z Z
Z
Z

3 p.m.: We tried **fetch** . . .

4.45 p.m.: Turns out Gnasher is great at swinging from the curtains . . . when he's told to 'SIT!'

5.15 p.m.: We tried playing dead . . .

Maybe he's playing someone who popped their clogs on a roundabout?

I'd never realized how naughty Gnasher was . . .

Ha! That's my boy!

5.37 p.m.: He just gnawed the leg off a table when Olivia told him to 'BEG!'

BEG! I SAID BEG ... BEG!

OBEY!

Haha! When I first arrived at the Perfect Pooch Pavilion this morning, I was sure I would have shrivelled up into a Boredom Mummy by now.

HOW WRONG WAS I?

Watching Gnasher in obedience class was a **LAUGHTER-FEST!** HE REALLY IS A BUNDLE OF JOY AFTER ALL . . .

MENACING JOY!

I'm not sure the trainer agreed with me, but hey, that's what you get for trying to change a dog that's already perfect

. . . HA!

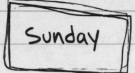

Sunday

Right!

This is our last chance to practise loads and prove to **The Fame Factor** judges at the town hall tomorrow that we're the only possible winners. It's the best way to reach the live **final** at Beanotown TV Studios and get the chance to play our **ROCK** to the whole world . . .

I'd better be off, my **Trainée Menaces**. I've got far too much to do and can't spend the day writing in this notebook.

Don't worry, I'll fill you in on how it goes . . . but you can bet that today's rehearsal will look **something like this . . .**

9 a.m.:

Today's the day, my **Menacing Mates!**

I can't wait to show Beanotown just what the Dinmakers are made of and, thanks to my trusty Mega-Bleep-Digi-Clock, me and the boys are up early and ready to transform ourselves into

KINGS OF ROCK!

It's easy if you know how . . . I just need to get my hands on a few bits and pieces to become an instant ROCK MENACE!

RULER OF ROCK!
Things I'll Need:

One of Dad's old golfing gloves

Hair spiked with Mum's super-strong hairspray

Bea's face paints are always handy

Gran's old leather motorbike jacket

The guitar Gran bought me on my birthday

POWER STANCE!
It's all about posing with your feet really wide

10 a.m.:

Me, Curly and Pie Face are about to set off to the town hall. **Ha!** I've just seen Walter waving goodbye to his mum and dad in his goblin get-up. He hasn't got a clue what he's getting himself into . . .

Beating my archest enemy is going
to be the most fun **EVER**. Walter
always thinks he's better than
everyone else . . . I can't believe
I'm saying this, but I suppose I can't
blame him. At school, he is. Well,
Mrs Creecher and Headmaster think
he is anyway . . . In term time at
Bash Street School, the teachers
LOVE Walter **SO MUCH**
and he comes top of the class in
everything. It's no wonder he's such a

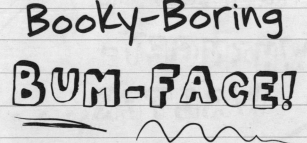

Booky-Boring
BUM-FACE!

But we're not at school now and there's not a teacher in sight. The guest judges on **The Fame Factor** are bound to be super cool! I bet they'll run away, screaming

'I'M GOING TO DIE OF BOREDOM-BRAIN-ROT!'

when Walter and his cronies walk on.

BRAIN

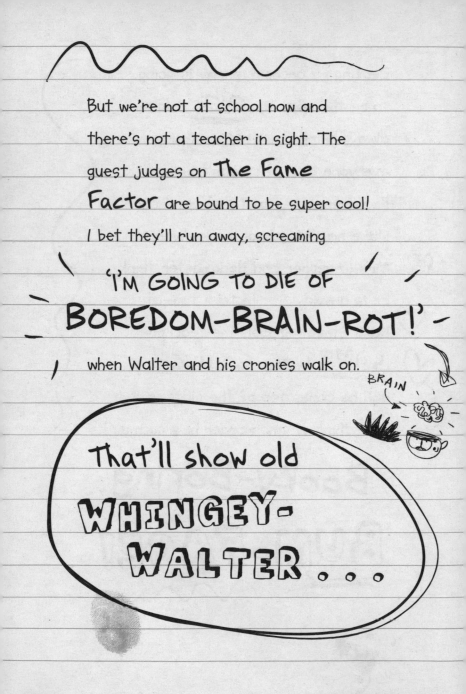

That'll show old

WHINGEY-WALTER ...

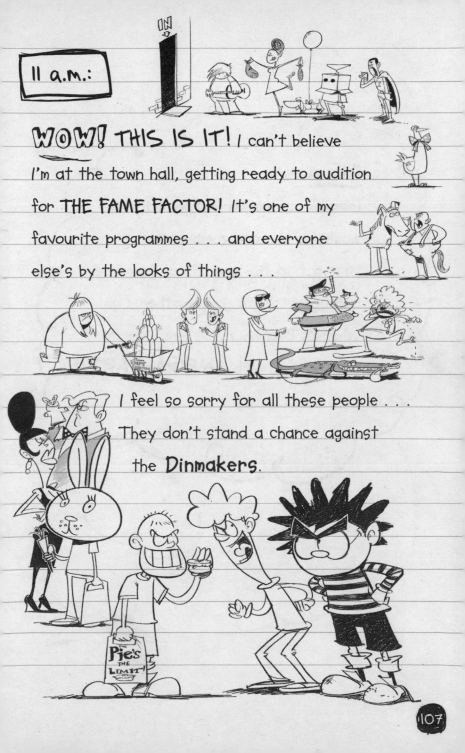

11 a.m.:

WOW! THIS IS IT! *I can't believe*

I'm at the town hall, getting ready to audition

for **THE FAME FACTOR!** *It's one of my*

favourite programmes . . . and everyone

else's by the looks of things . . .

I feel so sorry for all these people . . .

They don't stand a chance against

the **Dinmakers.**

THE Pie's THE LIMIT!

107

11.15 a.m.:

Hmmmm . . . I never imagined there would be so much queuing. We've just got to the end of one long line and been told to join another. Ugh! Where's Bea when you need her to clear a path with a **MEGA-FART**?

I can't wait to get out there and show
the judges how amazing we are. They're
bound to love our music and put us
straight through to the live final.

WATCH THIS
SPACE,
MY MENACING MATES...

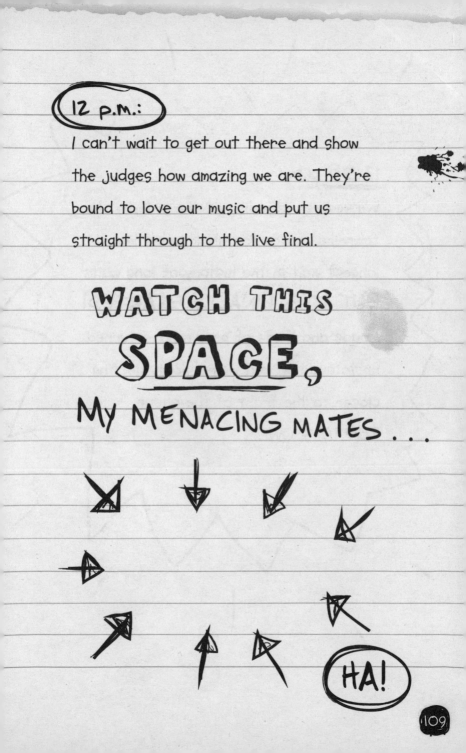

HA!

12.30 p.m.:

We've been standing at the side of the town-hall stage for what seems like the longest wait in the history of long waits, **BUT IT'S FINALLY STARTED!** Loads and loads of people have turned up to audition and we're slowly getting closer to the front of the queue . . . REALLY SLOWLY!

1 p.m.:

Me and the boys are nearly there!

~~I'm quite nervous.~~

I'M NOT NERVOUS AT ALL!

NO!

NEVER!!!

It's been fun watching the other acts from offstage, though . . .

Minnie the Minx did a roller-skating

routine while blowing bubbles with her **Pucker-**

'N'-Pop bubblegum . . . That was pretty

impressive, but she didn't get through! The

judges must be crazy . . . those bubbles were

GINORMOUS!

HA-HAAA!

<u>Gran</u> performed the **LOOP OF DEATH** on her Charley Davidson motorcycle, with Gnipper and Rasher on the back. I was so proud . . .

BUT SHE DIDN'T GET THROUGH EITHER!?!?!?!

The Bash Street Kids made a human pyramid, but it didn't go very well . . .

They definitely didn't get through.

Bea shot tin cans off a fake wall from twenty paces away . . . but she didn't get through. Are the judges not watching? That was some of the highest-quality **MEGA-FARTING** I've ever seen!

Then something strange happened.

Mrs Creecher recited her twelve times table while speed-marking homework and giving a wide range of disapproving glares all at once.

372 × 12 = 4,464

Don't ask me why, but the panel seemed to love that one . . . I wonder who the mystery guest judges are? They put her through to the **live final** on TV!

- Mrs Creecher!?

Something weird is going on . . .

3 p.m.:

<u>HA</u>! I never imagined today would turn into one of my biggest menaces ever.

IT WAS GENIUS!

Me and the Dinmakers are through to the live final.

YEAH!

Not without a bit of trickery and menacing genius, though.

You won't believe what happened, my Trainee Menaces. It was a seriously close call.

Walter, Dudley and Bertie had just wafted through all twenty-five minutes of the Dance of the Salty Prune Goblin and most of the audience were busy snoring loudly or sneaking off to the snack machines. IT WAS SO **BORING**. But . . . I couldn't believe it . . . the judges **LOVED** it. They actually **LOVED IT!!!**

I could hear them **WHOOPING** and **CHEERING** and they sent the Softies straight through to the live final.

I knew then that something was wrong. **REALLY WRONG!** I tried to rack my brains to think what it could be, but . . . that was when they called us up onstage.

There was lots of clapping and cheering from the crowd in the town hall . . . Imagine how pleased they must have been when Walter and his moaning minions were finally gone and a new MENACE-TASTIC act was about to entertain them!

I couldn't see very much at first because of all the bright lights. Then I spotted the two usual **Fame Factor** presenters . . .

SIMON SCOWL   GLITZY McTWINKLE

But I couldn't quite get a look at the three special guest judges . . . The lights were just too bright.

THEN . . . Just when me and the Dinmakers were about to leap into 'INTERGALACTIC GRANNY!' and blow everyone's bonces off, the spotlights dimmed and I saw the three judges . . .

My jaw nearly hit the floor and rolled away. Of all the worst people in the WORLD to judge ROCK MUSIC . . .

This next bit is seriously

SHOCKING!

The judges were . . .

HEADMASTER,

the BEANOTOWN
BUTTERFLIES
TROOPMASTER

and the . . .

LIBRARIAN FROM

BEANOTOWN LIBRARY!

Those wrinkly old **BUM-FACES** were the secret judges! **WHO** chose **THEM?** It was TERRIBLE! Like a circus of BOREDOM! How can three of the most BUM-FACIEST people to plod across the face of the earth judge an exciting talent show? It was **MADNESS**!

In a flash, I saw everything that was about to happen . . . sort of like a really, **REALLY** boring film in my head. I saw me and the boys playing amazing **ROCK** music. I saw the crowd going wild with excitement . . . AND I saw the three judges shaking their heads and pulling sour faces. Bum-faces like that would NEVER like the Dinmakers. There was no way we'd get through to the final if we played

'INTERGALACTIC GRANNY!'

in front of that lot.

123

Even though it's probably the best song ever
written . . . probably . . .

What were we going to do?

All three of the judges HATED me.
The Troopmaster says I'm a Menace cos
I flattened the new Beanotown Flower Gardens
on my **Rapid Reaper machine.**

The Librarian has always had her beady eye on me and it's her favourite hobby to **SHHHHHH** me if I ever make a sound . . . AND . . .

Headmaster is still grumpier than a bull with bellyache about me locking him in the staff toilets on World ~~Book~~ Menace Day.

I could see them all waiting for me and the Dinmakers to play just one note of music before they threw us on to the rejection pile!

Thinking on my feet, I quickly whispered to Curly and Pie Face and, before Headmaster, the Troopmaster and the Librarian could even think about wrinkling up their noses and sending us off, we played 'TWINKLE, TWINKLE, LITTLE LIBRARIAN' instead.

(Ha!)

It was one of the first things we learned to play in music class when we started at Bash Street School.

They were gobsmacked!

Headmaster, the Troopmaster and the Librarian were so surprised to like our music they just stared for a moment and then put us through to the final!

Headmaster looked like he'd just swallowed a swarm of bees . . . It was **BRILLIANT** and so worth it!

OK, it wasn't too cool to play 'Twinkle, Twinkle, Little Librarian', **BUT WHAT DO I CARE?** So what if we didn't look like RULERS OF ROCK in the first round? No one bothers about the bit that isn't on TV, and anyway everyone in Beanotown knows that I'm

THE PRANKMASTER GENERAL!

Just wait until the **LIVE FINAL** comes around ... **ON TELEVISION!** The public get to vote for the winner of that show and, just when they think we're about to play nursery rhymes, we'll hit them with the coolest, CRAZIEST, MOST HEAD-BANGING MUSIC they've ever heard and win the **£1,000** easily.

There's no way anything can go **wrong** now!

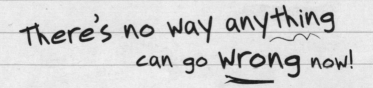

| Forget that last bit! |

It looks like we've got trouble, my
Menacing Mates.

I had just walked offstage and was
heading towards the exit with Curly and
Pie Face when I noticed Walter and his
cronies sneaking into one of the
dressing rooms.

At first, I thought it might be fun to creep
up behind them and jump out . . . They
always scream like Mum when she's seen a
mouse when I do that. **It's <u>HILARIOUS!</u>**

I was right behind the door when I heard Walter wail. He was SO angry . . .

No! Dennis CHEATED! I heard their rotten song when they were practising!

THEN I heard Walter say . . .

We'll get that HOOLIGAN, chaps. On live television. Just you watch!

UGH!

That's just what I need. Walter might be
a WHINGEY-WAFTY-WET-LETTUCE,
but he's a devious little smarmer at the
best of times. I'm going to have to keep
a close eye on my arch-enemy between
now and the live
final. Hmmm . . .

Thursday

I've got **one question** for you,
Trainee Menaces . . .

WHO IS THE GREATEST MENACE
OF THEM ALL?

ME!

I told you I was going to have to keep an
eye on Walter, didn't I? I've followed him
everywhere for the last few days. If I'm
honest, there were moments when I thought
I wouldn't make it . . . I really didn't!

Somehow, Walter manages to fill his days
with only the most, MOST, MOST

boring things a person can do . . . **BUT I GOT HIM!** I know what Walter and his snob-nosed chums are planning to do!

Here's what happened . . . **Super Spy Dennis** in action . . .

I followed him to the art gallery . . .

THE PHYSICAL IMPOSSIBILITY OF PICKLED SHARK ETC.

THAT'S POSSIBLY THE MOST RIVETING JUG AND TOMATO I HAVE EVER SEEN!

On a hike with his scout group, the

Beanotown Butterflies . . .

And even to **Beanotown Burgers** . . .
which was torture!

Everything seemed normal. I didn't spot
a single moment when Walter looked
like he was plotting to ruin the Dinmakers'
performance on **The Fame Factor**.
SO there was only one thing for it, my merry
band of Menaces . . . The oldest tried-and-
tested way of knowing what someone's up to . . .

I had to get my hands on <u>Walter's diary</u>!!!
But he NEVER takes it out of his satchel!

Lucky for us, I know that King Wafty-
Trousers goes to synchronized-swimming
classes on a Wednesday night. That was the
perfect place to pinch it.

Me and Gnasher stood by the big glass window
in the entrance hall of Beanotown Swimming
Baths — y'know, the bit where you can watch
the swimmers if you're too wimpy to take a dip
yourself — and waited for Walter to appear.

The minute he skipped out of the changing
rooms, ready for his class . . .

Gnasher was off!

He raced past the receptionist without being seen, into the boys' changing room and made straight for the cubicle where Walter had left all his stuff.

With Gnasher's amazing nose and Walter's unmistakable stink of books and bum, it was pretty easy for my best **pet-pal** to find it. GNNASH!

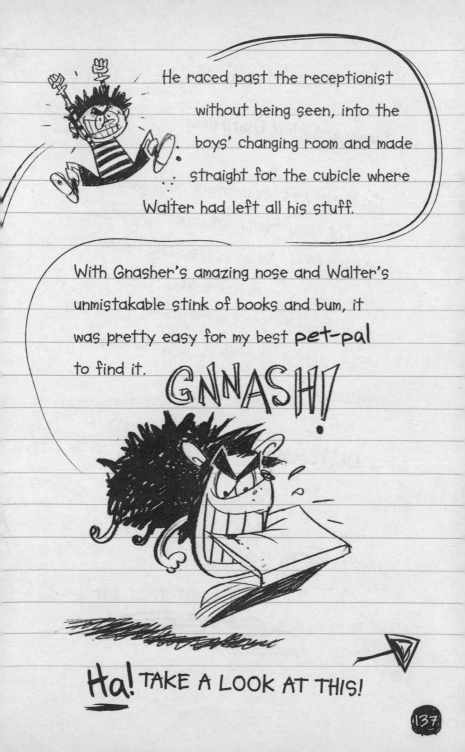

Ha! TAKE A LOOK AT THIS!

Dearest darling Diary dear,

I'm so nervous about tomorrow's audition for *The Fame Factor*, I'm practically all a shudder! The Dance of the Salty Prune Goblin is such a majestic piece. I'll be devastated if I don't perform with grace and dignity like my dadsie did when he was a young chap.

Oh! I could just cry!

<u>Erm</u> . . .

no . . . not that bit . . .

My dear Diary,

What a day it has been! Naturally, my friends and I were put straight through to the final round on *The Fame Factor*. With gifts of dance like ours, how could we not? I want to feel happy and skip through town with a smile and a song . . . but I don't!

Dennis, that dreadful guttersnipe I've told you about, got through too . . . only his horrid ROCK band didn't play what they were supposed to. Dadsie paid all that money to the boss of *The Fame Factor* to make sure the Troopmaster, the Librarian and Headmaster were the guest judges and it didn't work. I have to do something! I just have to! **Dennis the Menace will NOT triumph this time!**

What did I tell you? It gets even more interesting . . .

I've got it, my Diary-pal!

At tomorrow's live final, after Dudley, Bertie and I wow the audience with our magnificent dance, we are going to ruin Dennis's number. I know what he's planning, the brute. Everyone else may be silly enough to believe that Dennis and the Dinmakers are going to play nursery rhymes, but I'm not.

Before Dennis can let loose a single note, I'm going to turn the volume on the speakers all the way down and yank the button off so no one can turn it up again. Haha! It's brilliant!

Dennis will be humiliated on live television and never come out of his nasty little tree house again!

The End . . .

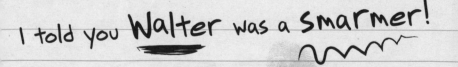

I told you **Walter** was a **smarmer!**

Oh, don't get all worried and start crying this close to the end, my Trainee Menaces. They don't call me the INTERNATIONAL MENACE OF MYSTERY for nothing, you know!

The minute I read what Walter was going to do, I concocted my own plan of attack. I wasn't about to let that Whingey-Wilfred stand between me and building **MENACE-OPOLIS** with my **£1,000** of prize money.

So here's what we're going to do . . .

If Walter wants to turn down the volume on all the speakers in the TV studio, he can . . . because we're not going to be using them.

I borrowed Mum's mobile and called my **MENACE-TASTIC gran**. She always knows what to do when there's a serious menacing dilemma.

Gran has a supercharged MEGA-loudspeaker of her own, called the **MEGASONIC 20K** . . . and she says we can borrow it for the live final.

Walter will bust his bunions when he sees the Dinmakers have outsmarted him.

Here goes, my Menacing Mates!

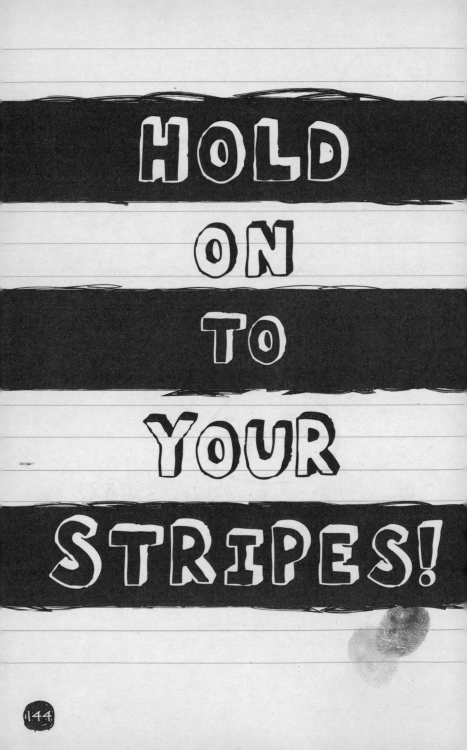

HOLD ON TO YOUR STRIPES!

144

7 p.m.:

Agh! I can't believe we're actually here! Inside the Beanotown TV Studios! The place is massive and there are cameras and people running all over with headsets and walkie-talkies.

This is going to be the best night of my life . . . I can just tell. The whole town is in the audience and out there, all around the world, people are settling down in front of their TVs, ready to watch me and my band

ROCK THE UNIVERSE!

The three finalists, Creecher, Walter and his cronies, and me and the Dinmakers are all backstage getting ready to do our stuff.

We've thrown one of Mum's old bed sheets over the **Megasonic 20K** to make sure that Walter doesn't see it until just the right moment. Gnasher is guarding it for now. He's such a good boy . . . Obedience training or no obedience training, he'll always be my bestest pet-pal.

AGH! I can almost see the gates of Menace-opolis rising up before me . . .

IT'S **SO** EXCITING!

7.30 p.m.: WE'RE OFF!!! Simon Scowl and Glitzy McTwinkle have just gone out onstage to start the show. **Phew!** I've got butterflies in my belly . . . Menacing, grizzly-type butterflies, of course . . .

7.35 p.m.: Walter, Dudley and Bertie are up first with their 'trotting troll' dance or whatever it's called. It's a great big snoozefest, that's for sure.

7.45 p.m.: Ugh! The Softies are still onstage, prancing about. This dancy thing goes on forever! The poor audience . . . I'll give them about another minute before . . .

Ha!

8 p.m.: Huh . . . Walter finally finished
the Dance of the Salty Prune Goblin.
I have to hand it to the Softies . . .
they're stubborn. Even with the audience
booing and shouting, they carried on and
finished the whole thing, which means
they're still in the competition.

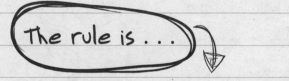

The rule is . . .

IF YOU DON'T FINISH YOUR

ACT ONSTAGE, YOU'RE

DISQUALIFIED!

8.05 p.m.: Now it's Mrs Creecher's turn . . .

WOW! She's really jazzed up her act. Creecher is still doing her twelve times table and speed-marking homework, but now she's wearing a spangly dress and feathers in her hair . . . and you should see those disapproving looks she's firing in all directions! She looks like a demented gurner on fast forward . . .

Ha!

11,369 × 12 = 136,428!

150

8.07 p.m.: Wait! Something's happened!

Creecher was in full flow when she . . .

Amazing! Ol' Mother Bum-Face was disqualified. That leaves just Walter and his cronies against us. This is too easy! There's no way we could lose against the Softies.

Haha! I can't help noticing that Walter seems to be shuffling around very close to the speaker-volume switches on the wall. I wonder why that is?

8.10 p.m.:

Here we go, my Menacing Marvels. This is it . . . the moment we've been waiting for. This is when I get my **£1,000** prize and you become fully trained Menaces just for being along for the ride.

LET'S ROCK!

152

9 p.m.: Sigh . . . What a night!

You should have been here . . .

The last fifty minutes were crazy . . .

We walked on to the stage and pushed the **Megasonic 20K** with the bed sheet over it into place. Then we picked up our instruments and were just about to reveal our big secret when . . .

WALTER LEAPT OUT ON TO THE STAGE, BRANDISHING THE SPEAKER-VOLUME CONTROL BUTTON LIKE A SWORD!!!

I think all this TV stuff had gone to Walter's
head. He turned straight to the camera and
said . . .

This band are a big bunch of
RAPSCALLIONS! They weren't
going to play you nursery
rhymes. They were going to
play noisy ROCK music. BUT I
STOPPED THEM!

I couldn't have asked for a better introduction!
It was AWESOME! I turned to Walter, struck
my power stance and said:

GUESS AGAIN
BUM-FACE!

That's when Gnasher whipped the bed sheet off the **Megasonic 20K** and cranked the volume all the way up . . .

157

For a minute, I didn't know what had happened until I managed to untangle myself from Curly and Pie Face. It was AMAZING! I felt like the greatest **ROCK STAR** that ever lived! I couldn't stop laughing until I realized . . .

OH NO!

NOOOOO!!! If we didn't finish our act, we were disqualified just like Creecher, but . . . but the **Megasonic 20K** had exploded into a squillion little pieces and Walter had broken the volume control of the TV studio speakers.

There was no hope . . .

Walter had won . . .

Ha!

You don't think us Menaces would have left old Whingey-Walter with the **£1,000** prize money, do you?

NEVER!!!

The whole place went silent as people slowly clambered back into their seats. Simon Scowl and Glitzy McTwinkle hobbled back onstage and were about to announce the Softies as the winners when something TERRIFIC happened. Gnasher bounded in front of the cameras and started doing all sorts of amazing tricks.

He rolled . . .

He jumped . . .

He walked on
his hind legs . . .

AND THEN HE HOWLED
THE TUNE TO
'INTERGALACTIC GRANNY!'!!!

161

The audience loved him! All the people watching the TV show from around the world voted for MY DOG! It turns out he'd listened to every word that poor old Olivia Pidd had told him at the Perfect Pooch Pavilion . . . He just hadn't been in the mood to obey . . . HA!

We went home that night happier than a Menace and his dog could ever be . . .

What a brilliant adventure this whole Fame Factor thing has been! I'm not even upset that I can't build Menace-opolis yet . . .

WHAT?

After all, it was GNASHER who won the contest, not me!

WHY NOT DO YOUR OWN MENACE JOURNAL?

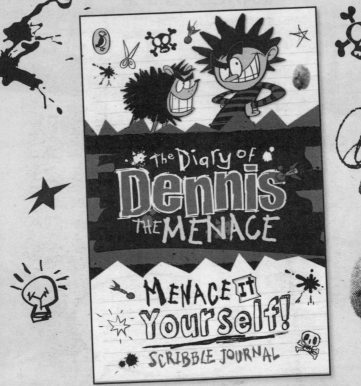

I've menaced my diary . . . now it's time to menace yours!

Join *The Beano* comic's front-page legend as he guides you through everything you need to know to create a book just like his. Your teacher will hate it!

COLLECT ALL THE BOOKS IN THE DIARY OF DENNIS THE MENACE SERIES!